CLEVER CUB
Is Amazed by God

Bob Hartman

Illustrated by Steve Brown

DAVID C COOK

transforming lives together

CLEVER CUB IS AMAZED BY GOD
Published by David C Cook
4050 Lee Vance Drive
Colorado Springs, CO 80918 U.S.A.

Integrity Music Limited, a Division of David C Cook
Brighton, East Sussex BN1 2RE, England

The graphic circle C logo is a registered trademark of David C Cook.

All Scripture paraphrases are based on the ESV® Bible (The Holy Bible, English
Standard Version®), copyright © 2001 by Crossway, a publishing ministry of
Good News Publishers. Used by permission. All rights reserved.

Library of Congress Control Number 2023939765
ISBN 978-0-8307-8594-0
eISBN 978-0-8307-8618-3

© 2024 Bob Hartman
Illustrations by Steve Brown. Copyright © 2024 David C Cook

The Team: Laura Derico, Stephanie Bennett, Judy Gillispie, James Hershberger, Karen Sherry
Cover Design: James Hershberger
Cover Art: Steve Brown

Printed in China
First Edition 2024

1 2 3 4 5 6 7 8 9 10

060223

Mama Bear and Clever Cub (along with Fred the bunny) traveled to the **SEA**. "Wow! It's **SO** pretty!" Clever Cub's eyes got big.

He looked all around. "Look at the waves! The sky! And all those puffy **CLOUDS**!"

Mama Bear smiled. "God made it all, and He made it all for us!"

"That's **AMAZING**!" The little bear jumped up and splashed in the water.

"Do you want to hear something even more amazing?" Mama Bear asked.

"From the Bible?" Clever Cub looked excited.

Mama Bear grinned. "You *are* a clever cub. Yes, from the Bible! It's a story about the sea, in fact."

"This sea in front of us?" Clever Cub scratched his nose. He was thinking.

"No-o-o, not exactly," Mama Bear said. "But one very much like it. It was called the Sea of Galilee.

"One day, Jesus told His friends to get into a **BOAT** and go across the sea to a town called Bethsaida (beth-SAY-duh)."

"Jesus did not go with them?" Clever Cub tugged on an ear. He always did that when he was worried.

7

"No-o-o, not at first. Jesus wanted to go up, up, **UP** on a mountain so He could have some quiet time to pray to God. He told His friends that He would catch up with them later."

"Oh, so Jesus had a boat?"
Clever Cub liked boats.

"No-o-o, not exactly." Mama Bear smiled as if she had a secret surprise.

She continued with her story. "Later that evening, Jesus looked out across the sea and saw that the wind was **PUSHING** against the boat. And His friends were **PULLING** against the oars. And the disciples were **SO-O-O** worried."

Clever Cub's eyes got very, very big.

"Just before dawn," Mama Bear continued, "Jesus went to meet His friends."

"But how? Did He **SWIM**?" Clever Cub tried to imagine Jesus in swimming trunks and flippers. He giggled out loud.

"No-o-o, not at all!" Mama Bear's voice got excited.
"He **WALKED** right out on top of the water!"

"Wha-a-at?!" Clever Cub was so surprised, he jumped up and knocked over Fred's seashell tower. "But that's **IMPOSSIBLE!**"

Mama Bear shook her head. "No, not for the One who made the seas and all that is in them.

"You see, the Bible tells us that Jesus was with God always, right from the beginning of the **WHOLE** world. So if Jesus could create something as amazing as the sea—"

15

"Then He could do something as amazing as walking on it!"
Clever Cub ran right into a big **WAVE** on the shore.

"Exactly!" Mama Bear nodded.

16

"But Mama, what did Jesus' friends do when they saw Him on the water? Were they **AMAZED** too?" the little bear asked.

"Well, not amazed exactly. At first, they were **TERRIFIED**!" Mama Bear's eyes got big. "They were so surprised, they did not even see that it was Jesus! They thought He was a ghost! But then He said, 'Do not be afraid!' And He climbed into their boat."

18

"And He made their boat go faster than ever?" Clever Cub imagined the boat racing across the Sea of Galilee.

"No. Instead, the wind stopped **BLOWING**. And the waves stopped **CRASHING**. And they were able to row all the way."

"And *that's* when they were amazed?" asked Clever Cub.

"Yes, then they were amazed," Mama Bear replied. "So every time you look out at the sea and are amazed by God's work, you can also remember the amazing thing Jesus did!"

"Now watch me, Mama! I'm going to make an **AMAZING** splash!"
And Clever Cub made his biggest jump ever into the water.

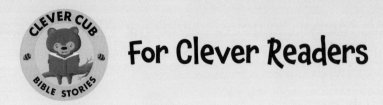

For Clever Readers

Clever Cub is a curious little bear who **LOVES** to cuddle up with the Bible and learn about God! Clever Cub thinks the sea is amazing! But Mama Bear reminds her cub that the Maker of the seas is even more amazing. You can read the exciting story of Jesus walking on the water in Mark 6:45–54.

Look around your world today. What do you see that is amazing? What do you see that is made by God? Although we may never see Jesus walk on the water, we can learn about all the amazing things God has done for us by reading His Bible stories. God knows you and loves you, and that's amazing too! What other amazing things can you thank God for today?